I Love You, MOMMY

igloobooks

I love you, Mommy,
because you cover me with kisses,
like warm sunbeams when I wake.

When we play hide and seek and I peek,
you say, "Boo! Found you,"
and you tickle me until I giggle.

Mommy, I love you because
when I tumble into muddy puddles, you
wash me and then make me warm and dry.

When I am scared, you are there to
hold out your arms and keep
me from harm and catch me when I fall.

I love you, Mommy, because you smell like summer flowers and are soft and snuggly like a bed made of feathers.

When snowy weather comes, you keep
me cozy and warm and we count
snowflakes falling from the sky.

Mommy, I love you because
you play with me all day and give me
hugs and treats and nice things to eat.

When the sun is low,
I sit on your lap and you rock and pat my
back and hum like happy honey bees.

I love you, Mommy, because you
show me the stars and the bright, round moon
and whisper to me, gently,
"Hush, now, shush now, settle down."

When it's time to say goodnight
and turn out the light, you make
the darkness glow with fireflies.

I love you, Mommy, because
you hold me close, as I drift off to sleep
and dream of how much you love me.

I love you, Mommy, because
you're *my* mommy.